SPOOKY SLEUTHS

Fire in the Sky

SPOOKY SLEUTHS

Read them all . . . if you dare.

SPOOKY SLEUTHS 4

Fire in the Sky

Natasha Deen

illustrated by Lissy Marlin

A STEPPING STONE BOOK™

Random House 🏠 New York

This is a work of fiction. Names, characters, places, and incidents either are the product of the author's imagination or are used fictitiously. Any resemblance to actual persons, living or dead, events, or locales is entirely coincidental.

Text copyright © 2023 by Natasha Deen
Cover art and interior illustrations copyright © 2023 by Lissy Marlin

Visit us on the Web!
rhcbooks.com

Educators and librarians, for a variety of teaching tools, visit us at
RHTeachersLibrarians.com

Library of Congress Cataloging-in-Publication Data
Names: Deen, Natasha, author. | Marlin, Lissy, illustrator.
Title: Fire in the sky / Natasha Deen; illustrated by Lissy Marlin.
Description: New York: Random House Children's Books, [2023] |
Series: Spooky sleuths; #4 | "A Stepping Stone book." |
Summary: "Asim suspects their new student teacher is Old Higue—a witch from Guyanese folklore—but Rokshar believes the woman has invented a new travel device."—Provided by publisher.
Identifiers: LCCN 2022014443 (print) | LCCN 2022014444 (ebook) |
ISBN 978-0-593-48896-6 (trade paperback) |
ISBN 978-0-593-48897-3 (library binding) | ISBN 978-0-593-48898-0 (ebook)
Subjects: CYAC: Supernatural—Fiction. | Folklore—Guyana—Fiction. |
Guyanese Americans—Fiction. | LCGFT: Novels.
Classification: LCC PZ7.1.D446 Fi 2023 (print) | LCC PZ7.1.D446 (ebook) |
DDC [Fic]—dc23

Printed in the United States of America
10 9 8 7 6 5 4 3 2 1

This book has been officially leveled by using
the F&P Text Level Gradient™ Leveling System.

Random House Children's Books supports the
First Amendment and celebrates the right to read.

For my siblings, who made growing up both spooky and spectacular —N.D.

To my family. Thank you for your support. —L.M.

1

It was Saturday afternoon, and falling snow made the ground slick. I held on to my backpack and walked carefully, excited to meet my friends Rokshar Kaya, her brothers—Devlin and Malachi— and Max Rogers. No way was I going to fall, hurt myself, and miss our first-ever sleepover at Max's house!

We were having a monster-movie night. Those films creeped me out, but since my family had moved to Lion's Gate, Washington, I was getting used to creepy!

This town was the spookiest place ever. There were voices that came across the water and shadowy figures moving in the forest. Rokshar thought the scary things were because Eden Lab, where our parents worked, had lots of secret projects. She figured sometimes science went wild. Max and I thought the spooky things were because of supernatural creatures.

As I walked, sunlight flickered between patchy clouds and lit up the sidewalk. *Wait a second.* The light was red, not yellow. I looked up. It wasn't the sun darting between the clouds. It was a bright red fireball! A trail of black smoke followed its path. The fireball disappeared behind the row of abandoned houses.

I waited for a *boom* as it hit the ground, but everything stayed quiet. That chilled my whole body. There was only one thing to do. I swallowed my fear and went to investigate.

Cautiously, I moved forward. A plume of smoke rose from behind a red house with broken front steps. The front door creaked on rusty hinges. Dead trees and bushes crowded the lawn.

"Yeah," I muttered, "not creepy at all." As I turned toward the back of the house, a scent wafted my way. It smelled like the time Dad burned the meat loaf. But another aroma tickled my nose, too. Copper. I spotted a hole in the ground with smoke rising out of it. I took a step, then slipped on ice. The sky was the last thing I saw before the world tumbled in front of me.

When I opened my eyes, I found myself at the bottom of the hole, staring up at the wintery clouds. I stood, wincing at the pain in my arm, and brushed myself off. The walls were smooth and slippery. And warm. *That's super weird.*

I searched for a way out, but I was stuck.

Suddenly, a shadowy figure loomed over me. I squinted, but I couldn't see who it was. I said, "I fell in the hole," then felt silly. That was obvious.

The person didn't say anything, but they didn't move, either.

It looked like they were wearing a long

coat. "If you hang your jacket over," I said, "I can use it to climb out of here."

The person stayed quiet.

The silence grew edges and poked me. My heart beat triple-time. "Okay," I said, hoping I sounded confident, "I'll call my folks to come get me." I *really* hoped the person would leave. I didn't want them to know that I didn't have a phone.

The person stood motionless for a long

moment. Then, in a whirl that sounded like the flapping of birds' wings, they spun from view. I exhaled in relief, then stopped. I was still trapped in a hole. Plus, I couldn't call for help. Not if the person was still there.

I blew on my fingers to warm them up. My friends would come looking for me when I didn't show up at Max's house. Which meant Mom and Dad would come looking, too. Then I'd be a fried banana when they realized I'd broken the town's rule that no one was to go near the abandoned houses.

Above me, there was a slithering sound. It got closer. I backed up against the wall and hoped it wasn't a snake. A second later, the end of a rope slid into the hole. I tugged and it held. I scrambled free. When I emerged, I was alone. I looked over my shoulder at where the hole had been. But it had closed up behind me. The lawn looked normal. There was only me, gasping for breath and certain that something terrible had landed in my town.

2

"Goodness!" said Ms. Rogers when she opened the door. She eyed the dirt on my clothes. "Asim, what happened?"

"I fell," I said, and stepped inside.

"You poor thing," she said. "I'll make some hot chocolate. That'll get you warm."

I cleaned up and changed into my pajamas, then met my friends in Max's room.

"Did you really fall?" asked Malachi, brushing his dreads off his forehead. "Or did you run into something spooky?"

"Both," I said. "I fell into a hole behind one of the abandoned houses."

Max's blue eyes went wide. "What were you doing there?"

I told them what happened.

Devlin hugged his thin frame. "Those houses are creepy. I bet you saw a ghost. They're just air; that's why it couldn't help you."

"Then who threw the rope down for him?" asked Rokshar.

Devlin's cheeks puffed out. "A helpful ghost with telekinetic powers."

"A ghost that can move things with its mind?" Max hid under a blanket. "That's worse than a regular ghost!"

"Did you write it down in your journal?" Rokshar asked me.

She and I had been keeping a record

of all the spooky things we ran into. "Not yet," I said, "but I will."

Rokshar moved to the computer and pulled her purple hair into a pony-tail. "The fireball is weird. So is the hole spontaneously closing up." She started typing.

We watched over her shoulder. She tried different search terms, like "glowing ball in Lion's Gate" and "meteorite hole closing," but she didn't have any luck. "There's only one thing we can do."

"Pretend it never happened?" Max said hopefully.

"No," she said. "We investigate. Monday, after school."

Max groaned. "I was afraid you'd say that."

Sunday night, before bed, I opened my journal. Step one of the scientific process was to ask a question.

A glowing ball of fire appeared in the sky and landed behind the row of abandoned houses. What was it? How did the hole disappear so quickly?

I pulled up my socks, then added:

I fell into the hole. Why were the sides warm and smooth?

I had a lot of guesses. The fireball might be a meteorite, space junk, something supernatural, or an alien ship. Step two of the scientific process was to form a hypothesis. But there were too many options for just one. I climbed into bed.

The next morning, I had breakfast with my parents.

"Do you want a slice of toast?" asked Dad, holding up a bag of bread.

"No thanks," I said.

"But it *loafs* you," he said.

Mom and I groaned.

"I'm going to school," I said.

"So early?" Mom asked, checking her watch.

"Uh, yeah, I'm going to hang out with my friends before the bell," I said.

"Hmm." She gave me a suspicious look but let me go.

I left to find some clues about the fireball. I turned the corner and saw a lady standing in front of the same abandoned house where I'd been on Saturday.

Her long black hair blew in the wind as she scanned the upper floors. She started for the porch.

"Wait!" I called. "It's not safe!" But I was too far away. She couldn't hear me. I sped along the icy sidewalk, looking down to avoid the slippery bits. When I got to the walkway that led up to the house, the lady had disappeared.

I went to the back of the house, but she wasn't there. A creepy-crawly feeling slithered along my neck. I wanted to bolt, but what if the lady was in trouble? I retraced my steps. There were no footprints leading to the door. *At least she didn't go inside,* I thought, relieved. *That would have been dangerous!*

Dread filled my body as I realized that there were no footprints anywhere, except for mine.

I got to school just as the final bell rang.

"Cutting it close," said Mx. Hudson as I scurried into the classroom. They smiled, so I knew I wasn't in trouble.

I hurried to my desk. Rokshar sat across from me, and Max was behind her. I told them what had happened. "Who doesn't leave footprints in the snow?"

"Ghosts," Max said.

"After school," whispered Rokshar, "we'll investigate."

"I have a special surprise for you all," said Mx. Hudson as someone knocked on our classroom door. "You're going to love it."

I hated it when adults said that. They were never right.

3

I jerked upright as someone walked into the room. "That's the lady from this morning," I whispered to my friends. "Probably Saturday, too!"

"This is Ms. Nazima!" said Mx. Hudson. "She is a physicist and a botanist. She's here as a student teacher for the month."

"I've always wanted to teach kids—I love children." Ms. Nazima smiled, but the way she spoke made me shiver. She caught me staring at her. Her eyes narrowed, almost like she recognized me.

Mx. Hudson started our math unit. When it was time for us to work independently, both teachers helped the class. But Ms. Nazima never helped me. Even if I was the only kid with my hand up and Mx. Hudson was busy, she ignored me.

But she was *really* focused on Max. She kept circling back to him. Once, I caught her leaning over him and inhaling. She got the same smile on her face that Mom wore near fresh bread. Was it the way Max smelled that had gotten Ms. Nazima's attention?

The back of my neck prickled with unease.

When the bell rang for recess, everyone scrambled to get outside. Except me.

I marched over to Ms. Nazima to get some answers. Kind of. My legs were doing their overcooked noodle impression, but I kept going.

"Ms. Nazima, I think I saw you at the abandoned houses this morning. On Saturday, too." I watched for her reaction.

She dipped her head. Her hair swung forward and hid her face.

Did she do that on purpose so I can't see her expression? I wondered.

Ms. Nazima looked up and laughed. "Gosh, no," she said. "Those houses give me the creeps."

I went to the coat rack, where Rokshar and Max were waiting. "No luck," I said. "I couldn't get an answer about this morning."

"Enjoy your recess," Mx. Hudson said to us. As Mx. Hudson walked toward the door, they said, "See you in the teachers' lounge, Ms. Nazima." They left.

While I bent to pull on my boots, Rokshar dug into her bag for her snack. I finished, straightened, and caught Ms. Nazima watching Max. Only, she was staring at him the same way Max's dog, Toby, stared at treats.

Goose bumps erupted along my skin. As she started our way, I grabbed Max and pushed him behind me. I smiled at Ms. Nazima. "We're going."

She moved to the door, waiting for us to leave so she could lock up.

As I hustled Max and Rokshar past her, a scent drifted my way.

Copper.

"She's definitely the same woman I saw!" I told my friends.

Max frowned. "If that's true, why didn't she help you out of the hole?"

"She did," said Rokshar. "She must have thrown down the rope."

I shivered as a gust of wind slipped

down my neck. "But why didn't she talk to me?"

"Those houses are off-limits to everyone," said Rokshar. "I bet she didn't want to get in trouble for investigating the fireball. She's a physicist, remember? I bet she has lots of ideas about it."

I nodded, but I wasn't sure Ms. Nazima could be trusted. Especially with the way she'd looked at Max.

The bell rang, and we headed to class. Max pulled ahead, and I tugged on Rokshar's arm.

"I didn't want to scare Max," I said, "but Ms. Nazima kept smelling him. She was looking at him the way your brothers look at dessert."

Rokshar's eyebrows rose. "I noticed that Ms. Nazima wouldn't help you during independent study," she said, "but she was always around Max. Let's observe her. We'll compare notes after school."

I watched Ms. Nazima for the rest of the day. During quiet time, I wrote down more questions in my journal.

Ms. Nazima was the person I saw on Saturday and this morning, because she has the same coat and she smells like copper. What is her connection to the fireball and the houses? Why does she look at Max like he's dinner?

"Be free!" said Mx. Hudson at the end of the day. "And think of poor Ms. Nazima and me. We'll be stuck here for our teachers' meeting."

Rokshar, Max, and I met up with Devlin and Malachi and headed to the abandoned red house. When we walked around to the back, we froze, hearing branches and twigs breaking.

"Someone's here," Malachi whispered. "Get behind us." He and Devlin took the lead. We crept to the edge of the house and crouched down, then peered around the corner.

I couldn't believe what I saw.

4

"Ms. Nazima!" I whispered. "We left school before her. How did she beat us here?"

"A shortcut?" Max suggested.

"There aren't any shortcuts to these houses from the school," said Devlin.

Ms. Nazima paced back and forth. Occasionally, she crouched and raked at the grass with her fingers. She stopped, then moved away from us.

When she disappeared around the side

of the house, we went after her. We got to the corner and peeked around it.

She was gone.

I looked for her, but all I saw was my friends with confused looks on their faces.

Ms. Nazima had disappeared into thin air.

"Maybe she ran really fast," said Devlin, taking off his beanie and scratching his head.

"Maybe she's not human. What if she's an alien, and the fireball is her ship?" Malachi wondered.

"We'll need evidence to prove your theory," said Rokshar. "Maybe we'll find answers in the backyard."

Rokshar walked to one of the spots where Ms. Nazima had raked her fingers. She took an empty container out of her backpack and scooped some grass into it. "I'm going to run a few tests."

When I got home, I added my observations to my journal.

Even though we left school before Ms. Nazima, she beat us to the house. She was digging in the grass. Was she looking for the hole? Then she seemed to disappear into thin air. How did she move so quickly?

If she was an alien, maybe the fireball was her ship. Then again, if she was a vampire, that might explain her quickness. But vampires can't go out in daylight or they burn up.

Frustration made me itchy. I didn't have a hypothesis about what she was or what her connection to the fireball was. All I had were questions.

Mom and I had been collecting stories about supernatural creatures. The only difference between us was that Mom thought they were just fun, but I knew they were real. I scanned one of the books for fire-based supernatural creatures. I found one about a phoenix—I didn't think Ms. Nazima was one of those, but she might have been a dragon.

I closed my book and went downstairs to help Dad with dinner. We finished making tacos just as Mom got home from the lab.

"Mom, can vampires go out in daylight?" I asked as we sat at the table.

"I don't think so," she said. "Why?"

"I was reading through our stories, and I was curious," I said. "I wondered if there was a supernatural creature that could move really fast and also had fire abilities. I know about dragons and phoenixes."

"I can't think of any others offhand. We can check the books later," said Mom.

That night I lay in bed and added my hypothesis.

> Ms. Nazima is a supernatural creature, and she's connected to the fireball.

If I found evidence of her connection, then I'd know I was correct.

"Bedtime," Dad said. "Tomorrow's a big day."

I frowned. "Why is it a big day?"

Dad's face went as red as his hair. "Don't tell your mom I spilled the secret. Mx. Hudson's got a fun surprise for your class. You're going to love it."

Yeah, I really hated it when adults said that. They were never right.

5

The next morning, I told Rokshar, Devlin, Malachi, and Max what Dad had said about a surprise.

"I wonder what it might be," said Rokshar. "We should be prepared for everything."

I shared my hypothesis about Ms. Nazima being a supernatural creature and maybe being a dragon. "Step three of the scientific process is finding evidence. So I have to look for proof."

"Dragons like gold and treasure," said

Malachi. "Maybe she has a secret stash in a cave."

"That will take forever to find," said Max.

Devlin pulled out some coins. "Try this. Dragons love money."

"Right! She won't be able to resist taking it," I said. "Thanks!"

"Most people will take money if you give it to them," Rokshar pointed out.

"That's true, but dragons' eyes glow when they see treasure." I closed my fingers around the coins.

When we got to the classroom, Ms. Nazima was at her desk.

"I have to figure out a way to get the

money in front of her without making it obvious," I said to Max as I pulled out the coins.

"Good luck," he said.

I walked toward Ms. Nazima. My brain whirred, but I couldn't think of an idea. Someone bumped me from behind. I stumbled, and the coins fell out of my hands onto Ms. Nazima's desk.

"Sorry!" said Max in a loud voice. "I didn't mean to spill your money!"

"Genius!" I whispered to him. Then I turned to the desk and saw Ms. Nazima picking up the coins.

"Here you go," she said in a bored voice. "Be careful when you're walking, Max."

I stared at her, checking to see if her eyes glowed.

She frowned at me. "Yes?"

"Nothing," I said.

"You missed a coin," Max said. He bent over the desk and picked it up. As he did, Ms. Nazima's eyes went red. She leaned over him and inhaled. A dangerous smile curled her lips.

I grabbed Max. "Sorry again, Ms. Nazima!"

We hurried back to our desks.

"Did you spot anything?" Max asked.

"I'll tell you later," I said.

Mx. Hudson took attendance. They swept their hands toward Ms. Nazima and said, "Remember how I told you Ms. Nazima used to be a botanist? Tomorrow, we're going on a field trip to the forest, where Ms. Nazima will teach us about our town's plants. Your parents and guardians have already signed the permission slips." They winked at me. "Especially your dad, Asim. He loves the outdoors!"

So *that* was the surprise Dad had mentioned! Everyone murmured with excitement. Worry chewed my insides. What was Ms. Nazima planning, and why was she taking us into the forest? Did it have a connection to the way she looked at Max?

Throughout the day, I tried to

concentrate on my work. But I kept thinking about Ms. Nazima.

Mx. Hudson noticed. As the final bell rang, they said, "Asim, not every day is a great one. But tomorrow we'll be talking about exponential growth. I need you to focus."

I nodded, then went to the coat rack, where Rokshar and Max waited. Mx. Hudson held out a container to Ms. Nazima and said, "Would you like some fries?"

"Thank you," said Ms. Nazima. She ate one, then doubled over, coughing.

"Sorry!" said Mx. Hudson. "Is there too much salt?"

"It's fine," she said, pounding her chest.

My gaze went to Ms. Nazima's fingers. They had turned red. I nudged my friends and whispered, "Red fingers from touching salt. Coughing from it."

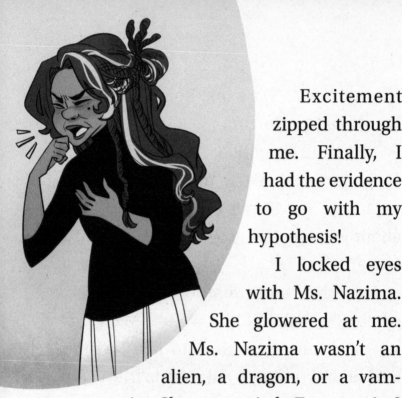

Excitement zipped through me. Finally, I had the evidence to go with my hypothesis!

I locked eyes with Ms. Nazima. She glowered at me. Ms. Nazima wasn't an alien, a dragon, or a vampire. She was a witch. Even scarier? From the look on her face, she knew that I knew her secret.

"A witch?" said Devlin as we all walked home together.

"Witches don't like salt," I said. "Plus . . .

she keeps smelling Max and looking at him like Toby looks at her treats." I turned to Max. "When you bent over her desk this morning, her eyes turned red and she looked . . . hungry."

Max went pale. "She wants to eat me?"

"We don't know yet," soothed Rokshar. "Maybe you remind her of a nephew or something." We stopped in front of the row of abandoned houses. "But if Asim is right, maybe it's your sweat she likes, Max. There's lots of research on the science behind perspiration."

"Gross," said Devlin.

Max's knees buckled.

"Let's take another look at the backyard," Rokshar said hastily. "There must be some evidence that can help us."

Devlin led the way.

"There's a circle where the grass is a

different color." Rokshar pointed. She cut out a small patch and put it in a container.

"Wait." I raised my hand. "Do you hear that?"

"It sounds like birds' wings," said Malachi.

"That's the same sound I heard when I was in the hole!" I said. "When Ms. Nazima turned away, her coat made that sound."

Rokshar looked over my shoulder. "Duck!"

I glanced back, then tackled Devlin as a ball of fire whizzed past us. The fireball arced into the air, spun around, and hurtled toward us again.

"Run!" screamed Malachi.

I sped for the forest and tree cover. My breath clouded the air, and the cold turned my lungs to ice. Heat warmed my back. The ball was behind me!

"Asim!" Malachi bellowed. "Run in a zigzag pattern! It'll be harder to get you!"

I took a sharp left, slipped, and smashed my knee on the icy ground.

The fireball zoomed by.

I scrambled upright as it rocketed past me.

"Use a tree for cover!" called Max.

I leaped behind one. There was a loud *crack* as the fireball blasted through the treetop.

"Try another one!" yelled Devlin.

I raced toward my friends.

"We're not trees!" Max shrieked.

There was no time to explain. I sped past them and ran to the street. If an adult was around, maybe they'd see and help.

The fireball chased me.

I was sweating, and my heart felt like it was going to explode. The whirring of birds' wings filled my ears. I slid onto the sidewalk. The fireball disappeared behind the house as a car came into view.

I collapsed on the ground, panting. The fireball had targeted me. My gut instinct said it wasn't going to stop until it got me.

The next morning was our field trip to the forest. Before we left, Mx. Hudson told us to have a snack.

Ms. Nazima held up a small container. She looked over at me. A creepy smile slithered across her face. "Mx. Hudson," she said, "would you like one of my pretzels? They're salty, just the way you like." She reached into the container and pulled one out. Holding my gaze, she said, "I love salt." She shoved the pretzel in her mouth and chewed. Her face puckered and her eyes watered.

"Are you okay?" Mx. Hudson asked.

"I'm great." Ms. Nazima's voice was raspy. She stared at me in triumph.

Witches don't like salt, I thought. Then something else occurred to me. *If she's not a witch, then why is she making a scene about the salt?*

As we lined up to leave for the field trip, Mx. Hudson said, "Students, form groups of three or four. A parent chaperone or teacher will join each group." They smiled at Elijah. "Your mom's excited for the trip."

Ms. Nazima came up to me, Max, and Rokshar. "I'll be your adult."

I flinched at the hungry smile she gave Max.

Rokshar raised her hand. "Mx. Hudson,

my wool cap has a rip in it. Can I go borrow one of my brothers'?"

They nodded.

Rokshar scurried out the door.

Elijah walked over to his mom as she came into the room. Ms. Nazima inhaled as he walked by her, and her eyes went dreamy, like she smelled something delicious.

Rokshar returned. She saw the concern on Max's face and hugged him. "Don't worry. I have a plan."

"Easy for you to say," he said. "You're not the one who might be a witch's dinner."

"Let's go!" Mx. Hudson led the way.

Rokshar and I exchanged determined looks. We weren't going to let anything happen to Max.

6

"Let's talk about symbiotic relationships," said Ms. Nazima as everyone crowded around her.

Being near Ms. Nazima made me shiver. So did the chilly, foggy air.

"That's when two things form a beneficial partnership, like trees and fungi," she said. "With your groups, see if you can find any examples of this. Chaperones, keep watch. The forest is beautiful but dangerous."

Everyone spread out. Soon, it was just us and Ms. Nazima.

I shivered again.

"I've been watching Ms. Nazima," Rokshar said quietly. "She's not acting strangely."

"I know," I said, feeling unsure. "Maybe I was wrong."

"Keep looking for an example of symbiosis," Ms. Nazima said. Her hand hovered near Max's shoulder. Her skin became wrinkly, and her face lengthened.

I swallowed my scream. I went to nudge Rokshar, but the student teacher's appearance returned to normal.

Ms. Nazima caught me staring. I smiled and pretended I hadn't seen her morph. My terror must have shown on my face, though, because her gaze narrowed. "Let's go this way," she said in a syrupy-sweet voice. She sped up and disappeared behind one of the trees.

"Why is she running?" Rokshar asked, and jogged after her.

I hurried, too, squinting to see Ms. Nazima through the fog.

She was gone.

Rokshar stopped beside me. "Where did she go?"

I turned around, and *Ms. Nazima was right behind us!* I yelped. "Where did you come from?" The scent of copper and burned meat loaf wafted my way.

"I've been here all along," she said.

"You need to stick close to me. You don't want to get lost, do you?"

Her smile made me nauseous.

"Wait a second," Rokshar said to her. "You're here. We're here." She looked around. "Where's Max?"

I took a breath to yell Max's name, when I heard a bunch of people yelling, "Elijah! Elijah!"

Rokshar and I looked at each other.

"Elijah?" I said.

Elijah!!

"Oh no," said Ms. Nazima in a fake-worried voice. "He must have gotten lost."

I frowned. As she led us to the group, I whispered to Rokshar, "Something spooky is going on. She vanishes, then reappears. At the same time, both Max and Elijah go missing." My frown got deeper. "It's spooky."

"It's not spooky," she said, frowning at Ms. Nazima's back. "I have a hypothesis, but—"

"Catch up!" Ms. Nazima called to us.

"I'll tell you later," said Rokshar.

"Elijah's missing," Mx. Hudson said when they saw us.

"He was right beside me," said Elijah's mom. She was crying. "Then, suddenly, he was gone!"

"Max is missing, too," I said.

Mx. Hudson looked sick.

"It's easy to get lost in the woods," Ms. Nazima said. "I'm sure we can track them . . . though the fog might make it difficult."

She sounds happy that we might not find Elijah and Max, I thought. Fear crawled along my spine and made my skin tight. *If she has my friends, what is she going to do with them?*

"We can find Max," said Rokshar. "My brother's phone is in Max's coat. I borrowed it, along with his hat." She smiled at Ms. Nazima. "The forest is beautiful but dangerous."

Ms. Nazima bared her teeth, then quickly formed a smile. "What great planning!" She moved to the back of the group.

"Max was carrying it for me," said Rokshar. "We can use it to track him."

"Wonderful! Ms. Nazima, do you—?"

Mx. Hudson's mouth fell open. "Where did she go?"

I turned around. Ms. Nazima had disappeared. Again.

"I'd say she's a ghost," I told Rokshar, "but she's got a solid form."

Rokshar scowled. "She's no ghost."

Suddenly, the noise of breaking branches made everyone turn. Elijah and Max came into view.

"Where did you go?" Elijah's mom said, scooping him up in a hug.

"Me?" said Elijah. "I was looking at the mushroom with you. Then you disappeared!"

"I did *what*?" said his mom.

"At first, I was scared. Especially when there was this weird sound and everything went dark. But then I spotted Ms. Nazima," said Elijah. "I followed her, and then I saw Max. We heard everyone's voices and walked toward the sound."

Max rubbed the back of his head. "That's kind of what happened. But I was behind Ms. Nazima." He glanced my way. "I heard the sound of birds' wings. Then everything went dark for a second. Suddenly, I saw Elijah. When I looked around, Ms. Nazima was gone."

"That's because I wasn't with either you or Elijah," Ms. Nazima said.

I jumped. *How did she appear beside me?*

"I was with Rokshar and Asim the entire time." She headed to Mx. Hudson. "Perhaps we should call it a day."

Mx. Hudson nodded.

"Did you notice how fast Elijah and Max got back to the group when Ms.

Nazima found out about the phone in Max's pocket?" I asked Rokshar.

"You must have put it there when you hugged me," Max said to her.

Rokshar nodded. "That was my plan. I didn't want to tell you and make you worry even more."

"I am worried, though," he said. "I *was* following Ms. Nazima, but then she disappeared, and I was all alone . . . until I saw Elijah." He shook his head. "It doesn't make sense. No way could she be in two places at once."

"Yes, she could," Rokshar said grimly. "And I don't like that one bit."

7

"Go ahead and take some personal time," Mx. Hudson suggested when we got back to school.

Rokshar, Max, and I went to the reading nook, where it was private. It was also next to Duchess. She was a yellow bearded dragon and our class mascot. I got permission from Mx. Hudson to feed her some sweet potatoes and mealworms.

"What were you saying before, about

Ms. Nazima?" I asked Rokshar after I'd finished.

"I ran tests on the grass samples," said Rokshar. "I found traces of diesel, copper ore, and plant oils, like canola and sunflower."

"What does that mean?" asked Max.

"Other than copper ore, all of those ingredients make biofuels," she said. "Copper is used as an electricity conductor. My hypothesis is that Ms. Nazima is experimenting with a new type of biofuel mixed with electrical energy. Remember what you said, Asim, about hearing birds' wings? I think that's the engine's sound."

I frowned. "Wouldn't an engine be big?"

"Maybe," she said. "But maybe Ms. Nazima has figured out a way for people to travel without needing a car or plane. She's a physicist, right?"

"So you think the fireball is a mode of transportation?" I said.

She nodded.

Max looked relieved. "This is much better than a witch who wants to eat me."

I wasn't convinced, but Rokshar had a good argument. "What do we do next?" I asked.

"The proof might be in her coat," Rokshar said. "She could have a book where she's keeping her notes. At lunch, we'll check her pockets."

After our break and before lunch, it was time for math. Mx. Hudson said, "Today, we're going to start our module on exponential growth. Max and Elijah, please hand out our supplies to the class. They're on Ms. Nazima's desk."

There were stacks of boxes with lids on top of them. Max and Elijah went over. Ms. Nazima barely noticed them. Max stumbled into her. Ms. Nazima caught him by the shoulders, but her hands didn't change like they had before. She didn't look at him like he might be food, either.

Am I wrong about Ms. Nazima? I raised my hand. "What's in the boxes?"

"It's a surprise," said Mx. Hudson.

Uh-oh. When Elijah put the box in front of me, I carefully peeled off the lid. My stomach churned as I thought of what Mx. Hudson's surprise might be. I peered inside, then laughed with relief. Looking to my teacher, who'd moved to stand beside Ms. Nazima, I said, "It's rainbow rice!"

Ms. Nazima startled, then cast a wary glance at the boxes on her desk.

Her actions tickled my brain.

"Do you like it?" Mx. Hudson said. "I dyed the uncooked rice in batches. We'll use the rice to visualize how quickly quantities grow when it's exponential growth."

"It's very pretty!" said Rokshar.

Mx. Hudson started teaching. I did my best to concentrate, but I was happy when the bell rang.

"Off to lunch!" said Mx. Hudson. "After you clean up."

Elijah rushed to put away his box. He tripped and fell. The box crashed to the floor, and rice spilled everywhere. "Sorry!" He scrambled to scoop up the grains.

Ms. Nazima kneeled to help.

"It was an accident, but a lesson to pay attention," said Mx. Hudson. "Elijah, borrow a broom from the custodian. It'll go faster than trying to pick them up grain by grain."

Elijah left, but Ms. Nazima kept picking up the rice. As she did, she muttered to herself.

My brain tickle turned into a full-on itch.

Elijah returned with a broom and went to the mess.

"Ms. Nazima," Mx. Hudson said. "Ms. Nazima! Elijah has a broom!"

"What?" she snapped. "Oh! Broom!" She straightened, then swayed.

Elijah caught her by the shoulder. The smell of copper and burned meat loaf wafted my way.

Fireball, Elijah, Max, nails, wrinkling skin, copper, burned meat loaf, and grains of rice. The solution to Ms. Nazima was so close, but I couldn't reach it.

I leaned toward my friends. "I don't know what Ms. Nazima is," I whispered, "but my gut says Max and Elijah are in terrible danger."

8

While everyone was distracted with helping to clean up the rice, Rokshar snuck over to Ms. Nazima's coat, but the student teacher noticed.

"What are you doing?" She strode over.

"I love your jacket," said Rokshar. She ran her hand along it. "What is the material? It feels like neoprene." She pointed at the design on the jacket. It was covered with small triangles. "This is so cool."

"Don't touch my things," Ms. Nazima

said sharply. She caught herself and gave Rokshar a sickly sweet smile. "Please."

Rokshar went back to her desk. When the teachers weren't looking, she whispered, "I took a sample of her coat. I'm going to get some answers!"

After dinner, Rokshar emailed us.

I knew something was up! I found bacteria, *Bacillus subtilis natto*, on her coat! It reacts to moisture—like sweat. If you were traveling in a fireball, you'd definitely sweat! I think Ms. Nazima uses the bacteria to keep her temperature down. I need more evidence, but I suspect her coat is a device that allows her to travel quickly. I'll have to investigate more to find out how the bacteria, sweat, and fireball work together.

I shut down the computer, then pulled

out the books on supernatural creatures. Rokshar's discovery was awesome, but I couldn't shake Ms. Nazima's strange reaction to the rice. I pored over every page of the books. When I found what I was looking for, my body felt like concrete. I had the answer to Ms. Nazima, and it was more terrifying than I had imagined.

The next day, as we walked to school, I told my friends what I'd learned.

"A witch?" Max frowned. "But she ate salt. Witches can't do that."

"She's not a regular witch," I said. "She's a Caribbean witch called an Old Higue. A combination of vampire and witch."

Max looked like he was going to faint. "A bloodsucking witch? I'm so dead!"

"That's your hypothesis, Asim," Rokshar said thoughtfully. "What's your proof?"

"One, the way she looked at Max. Two, the fireball—that's how Old Higues travel. Three, the rice," I said. "It's one of the methods you use to stop her. If you throw down rice, she's forced to pick up every grain."

"Do we just throw rice down everywhere we go?" asked Malachi.

"It *stops* her," I said, "but it doesn't *defeat* her."

Max groaned. "Please don't let me end up as her dinner!"

"If she's supernatural," said Rokshar, "then why did we find biofuel in the grass? That's a human-made substance. Plus the coat and the bacteria."

"But if she's just experimenting with a new form of travel," said Malachi, "then why did she take Elijah and Max?"

"I think she's seeing how much weight her jacket can handle and if it's capable of moving more than one person." Rokshar scowled. "It's not right to experiment with people without their permission." She dug in her backpack and pulled out some vials. Rokshar handed them out. "They're full of sand. If I'm right, and Ms. Nazima tries to take another kid, then throwing sand on the jacket might mess with the engine and the bacteria coating, and stop her."

I couldn't argue with that, but I couldn't shake my gut instinct, either.

Devlin nodded. "That's one option covered. What do we do about Asim's theory?"

"Old Higues leave their bodies when they travel in their fireball form," I said. "If we put salt and pepper on her body, she can't return to it. That will defeat her." I pulled out some containers. "Here, I mixed some up for each of us."

"We have a big problem," said Rokshar. "Ms. Nazima is smart. If she's an Old Higue, she'd never leave her body in a spot someone could find it. Where would she hide it?"

The five of us looked at each other.

At the same time, we said, "The abandoned houses!"

By the time I got to school, all I could think of was the final bell and getting to the houses. I was determined to discover the truth about Ms. Nazima. But it seemed that she was on to me and my friends.

After Mx. Hudson took attendance, Ms. Nazima went to the front of the classroom. "I have to leave because of a family emergency," she said. "I'm sorry to say goodbye."

Max leaned in and whispered, "Maybe we spooked her enough to stop her plan."

If he was right, this was great news! Ms. Nazima gave me a final scowl as she left. When she closed the door, the smell of copper came my way, and I had a terrible thought. *If the adults believe she's gone and a kid disappears, no one will suspect she's responsible.* My breath hitched and my heart beat triple-time. Ms. Nazima was going to make her move, but who would she take? Max or Elijah?

9

When the final bell rang, we met up with Malachi and Devlin. "I'm worried," I said as we walked home. "Ms. Nazima might be tricking us."

"Whether she was an Old Higue or a bad scientist, you got rid of her," said Malachi.

"Maybe. I'm glad Elijah's mom was there to take him home," I said. "If this is a trick from Ms. Nazima, at least he's safe."

"That leaves me," groaned Max. "I don't want to be eaten by Old Higue!"

Rokshar stopped. "Maybe it's not you, Max. Maybe she wants Asim."

"Me?" I squeaked.

"It might be supernatural or science. Either way, you wrecked her plans," said Rokshar. "If she's coming for a kid, it might be you." She tapped her chin. "Are you up for a risky plan?"

My legs did their overcooked noodle impression. "No," I said, "but if it protects the town, then yes."

"Walk home alone," she said, putting air quotes around *alone*.

I nodded.

After my friends left, I headed home. On the way, I passed the abandoned houses. I wanted to investigate again, but it wasn't safe to do so by myself. Reluctantly, I turned onto my street. My house came into view.

Just then, I heard the flapping of birds' wings. A thick, black blanket fell on top of me. I struggled to pull it off. Except it wasn't a blanket. It was heavy, dark air. I spun, trying to get away from it. Instead, I somersaulted, then hit the ground. The blanket disappeared. I found myself staring up at the menacing smile of Ms. Nazima.

"We meet again," she said.

I bolted upright, hoping to race for my house, then stumbled to a stop. We were behind the abandoned houses!

"You're all alone! There's no one to help you." Ms. Nazima lunged for me.

I dodged her, then ran for the main road.

I heard the sound of birds' wings behind me. The fireball blasted past; then Ms. Nazima appeared just ahead. I spun and ran the other way. She cackled. I spun again, but she kept blocking my path. I was getting dizzy and confused. How was she able to shift so quickly from a fireball to her human form? Could her body track her like a homing device? She stretched out her arm. Her fingers had become talons. I jumped out of reach, slid on the ice, fell, then scrambled to the protection of the woods.

She laughed again.

The high-pitched sound made my bones shake. My only hope was to run through the trees, then double back. As I ran, I reached into my pocket and pulled out Rokshar's vial. The back of my body got hot. *She's turned into the fireball!* I stopped, dropped to the ground, and felt the heat as she buzzed over me.

A plan formed in my mind,

but I needed to get her closer to me. I got to my feet but pretended I'd hurt my leg. Terrified, I watched as she morphed from the fireball back into her human form. She sped toward me. I waited until she was close, then threw the sand at her face.

Ms. Nazima screeched. She swiped at her cheeks. As she twisted away from me, the small triangles on her coat curled up like tiny horns.

I raced back toward the abandoned house. When I broke into the clearing, I saw my friends running in my direction!

Devlin and Malachi sped past, heading to Ms. Nazima.

"We got you covered!" Malachi shouted.

Ms. Nazima laughed. There was the sound of birds' wings, and then she disappeared.

"We have to get her coat!" Rokshar searched the sky for Ms. Nazima.

"How?" Devlin yelled back.

Rokshar pointed at me. "She wants Asim! We have to stay close to him!"

"Got it!" Malachi ran to me. So did Rokshar, Max, and Devlin.

"I have an idea!" I called.

Suddenly, the darkness surrounded me, but I was ready. I pulled out my container of salt and pepper. Closing my eyes and holding my breath, I shook the spices into the air.

There was a sputtering, coughing sound; then Ms. Nazima appeared in front of me. I lunged away, but she grabbed my ankle and hauled me to the ground. The spot where she held me burned. I screamed in pain.

"I'm not done with you," she growled. "I'm not done with any of you!"

Malachi and Devlin grabbed her arms and tried to pull her off. Ms. Nazima was too strong. They heaved and yanked, but they couldn't free me. "My backpack!" I yelled. "I have a bag of rice in there!"

Rokshar jumped on Ms. Nazima's back, grabbed her coat collar, and yanked.

I was losing strength. Ms. Nazima grinned as her face went long and lean. Her teeth turned razor sharp. I screamed and kicked.

From the corner of my eye, I saw Max dump out my backpack. He grabbed the bag of rice and poured the grains down Ms. Nazima's neck. Then he added the salt-and-pepper mix I'd given him.

Her shriek made my ears ring. "What have you done?" Ms. Nazima screamed. She threw Malachi, Devlin, and Rokshar off her. She stumbled to her feet.

Everyone threw sand, salt, and pepper at her.

Ms. Nazima screamed again and clawed at her body. Her body vibrated, then blurred. She began to shake.

"Take off the coat!" yelled Rokshar.

"We have to get out of here!" Malachi shouted. "Who knows where we'll end up when the coat blows?"

We raced for the sidewalk as her shrieks grew more terrible. The sound of flapping birds' wings made my eardrums vibrate. Ms. Nazima shrieked one final time, and then the air exploded around us.

Mom adjusted the blanket around me. She and Dad and my friends and their parents were gathered on the other side of the street. Someone had heard the explosion, seen the fireball burst into the sky, and called the emergency crews.

Mom thought my friends and I

happened to be on the street just after the explosion. I was okay with that. She'd never believe me about Ms. Nazima.

Dad hugged me tight. "I'm so glad you're okay."

"Those houses are old—they can catch on fire at any time. I don't know why the town hasn't torn them down," Mom said.

"Someone at the lab told me the houses were already on the island when Eden Lab bought the land. No one knows who built the houses or why they're still standing," said Dad.

Mom shivered. "That's spooky."

I bet Ms. Nazima knew, I thought. *She must have had a reason to visit the houses.* I didn't have the answer to that mystery. Plus, I wondered if the houses held a secret about how Ms. Nazima was able to hide her body but still rapidly

change from human to fireball form. I shuddered, wishing I had the answer, but there was no way to test that hypothesis. At least my friends were safe.

Mom put her arms around me. "These

houses are the kind of spooky things we like," she said to me, "but they're dangerous, and I don't want you exploring them."

"I *flame* to please," I told her.

My parents groaned.

I laughed.

Notes from Rokshar's Journal

- The strange occurrences with Ms. Nazima continue to puzzle me. Asim made good points about the student teacher's fascination with Elijah and Max, the way she "magically" appeared and disappeared, and her odd reactions to rice.

Sand??

Salt?

Rice??

Pepper?

Why kids??

- But my theory, that Ms. Nazima was working on a travel device, also fits. I found ingredients for biofuel and copper ore in the samples of grass that she touched. I also found a moisture-activated bacteria on her coat. Every time Ms. Nazima appeared

and disappeared, she was wearing her coat. The sound of birds' wings might have been the sound that the engine made. Ms. Nazima gave off the smell of copper. Could this be part of her new engine?

Biofuel?

CO_2

• However, there are things I can't explain. Why did she feel the need to involve children? What was the reaction between the sand, the rice, and her engine that caused the explosion? Where did she go?

• Conclusion: I cannot say whether Ms. Nazima was an Old Higue or if she was creating a new travel device.

Notes from Asim's Journal

* Ms. Nazima was an Old Higue, and I can prove it.

* She traveled in a ball of fire, she wanted to take Elijah and Max, and she tried to take me.

* Her skin, fingers, and teeth changed when she was around kids.

* I saw her turn from a fireball back into a human.

* When Elijah spilled the rice, she was forced to stop and pick up every grain. And when

Max poured the rice, salt, and pepper down her coat, it made her explode. But my biggest proof was seeing her turn from a fireball into a human being!

Need more salt and pepper!

Salt & pepper

Explode

Rice

* Conclusion: I'm positive my friends and I have saved the kids of Lion's Gate from a terrible fate.

Author's Note

If there was anything spookier than a witch and more terrifying than a vampire, it was an Old Higue. She was a combination of both! While most stories said Old Higue was an old woman, there were versions that had Old Higue as a man, too. Which made me wonder, could she also take the appearance of a young woman?

No matter what form Old Higue took, she was a horrifying creature. She liked to go after kids, and locking your door didn't help. Some stories said Old Higue could pour herself into one side of the lock, then out the other.

One of the best protections against this witch was leaving a pool of rice on the floor. Old Higue, the elders said, would be forced to pick up every grain. This gave you the chance to escape. In the past, when doors had old-fashioned locks and keys, there was another way to protect yourself: Turn the key halfway in the lock. If Old Higue tried to slip through the key-hole, she would get stuck.

Did Asim and his friends really defeat Ms. Nazima, or will she return for her revenge? Perhaps we should follow their lead and always carry vials of salt and pepper and rice with us!

WANT MORE STRANGE ADVENTURES WITH ASIM AND HIS FRIENDS?

Take a peek at

Spooky Sleuths: The Ghost Tree!

"That's a great idea." They grinned. "The land's been unused for the last two years. It's the perfect place to explore."

"It's dangerous," I blurted. "There are overgrown roots." *Plus, a creepy ghost tree that's eating the other trees, with leaves that make the shape of a skull.*

"Everyone knows the cemetery is haunted," Max said.

Mx. Hudson's expression grew thoughtful. "We're going to go there," they said, "and not just for the assignment. The cemetery isn't haunted. Those spaces allow us to honor our families." They smiled at Max. "You'll see, there's nothing to be afraid of."

I hated it when adults said that about supernatural things. They were always wrong.

"You shouldn't have suggested the grave-yard," Max said to Rokshar as we stood in the coatroom after school.

"Why not?" Rokshar said. "It's a great place for the assignment."

Max scowled. "You're putting us all in danger!"

He stomped away.

"What did Max mean?" I asked Rokshar as we left school. "When he said you're putting us in danger?"

She kicked a pebble and it skipped down the road. "There's something wrong with this town," she said finally. "You're new, so you probably haven't noticed, but strange things happen here."

"Like voices coming across the water when no one's around," I said. "Laughter when I'm all alone."

"You've noticed it, too?" she said. She made a face. "Max and my brothers think it's supernatural stuff and we should stay away."

"What do you think?" I asked.

"The lab," she said. "They run secret projects. That's why we're the only town on the island and why we're surrounded by ocean and mountains. I bet the strange stuff is the experiments getting out of control, and the scientists trying to fix them. It makes sense." She stopped. "At least, it would make sense if I could find proof."

"The lab does experiments with plants, right?" I asked.

"Right," she said.

That might explain the weird tree. I hoped it did. Wonky science was less scary than a ghostly tree.

"I have a bunch of journals," she said. "I've been recording stuff. Want to come over and see?"

"Tomorrow?" I said. "I have to get permission."

She nodded. "Deal!"

I was a couple of blocks away from her

when I reached into my bag for my house key. Oh no! It was gone! There was only one place I could have lost it.

The cemetery.

My folks were going to be irritated if I lost the house key. This was the first time they'd ever trusted me to have one. I had to go back.

I jogged to the cemetery, hoping the construction people were around. They'd be mad, knowing I'd been in the graveyard this morning, but maybe they'd help me find the key.

"Rokshar's right." I tried to convince myself. "It's just a science experiment that's run wild." Totally. Except I was so scared, I heard my heartbeat in my ears.

I got to the main gates, but I didn't see anyone. My legs did their overcooked noodles impression, but I went inside.

It was even spookier than I remembered. I tried to retrace my steps to where I'd lost my bag.

But each path looked the same as all the others. Soon, I was lost, and I found myself by the grove of dead trees. I crept forward, but I couldn't believe what I saw.

The ghost tree from this morning had grown. Now it was almost fourteen feet tall, with a thick trunk. The pool of black ink surrounding it was bigger, too. It slid along the dead grass and left burned

patches. The worst part was the dead trees around it.

This morning, they'd been leafless and cracked. Now they were bowed and bent. Their trunks looked like something had squeezed them. I heard moaning, as though they were in pain.

Stop it! I thought. *The moaning is probably the hum from the cables the construction team is putting in.*

Then I noticed an object shining on the cobblestones. My key. How did it end up so far from my bag?

The leaves of the ghost tree rustled, and it sounded as though it was laughing, daring me to come closer.

I pushed down my fear. *Don't be a coward!* I told myself. *It's just a tree!* As I moved toward it, I heard footsteps coming up the path, fast, heading straight for me.